I Don't Want to Go to Bed!

Based on the original stories created by
Ian Whybrow and Adrian Reynolds

PUFFIN BOOKS
Published by the Penguin Group: London, New York,
Australia, Canada, India, Ireland, New Zealand and South Africa
Penguin Books Ltd, Registered Offices: 80 Strand, London WC2R 0RL, England

puffinbooks.com

First published 2008
1 3 5 7 9 10 8 6 4 2

Made and printed in China
ISBN: 978–0–141–50172–7

Harry and his dinosaurs were bouncing on his bed.
Harry didn't feel in the least bit tired and he definitely
didn't want to go to sleep.

"It's nine o'clock," said Mum. "You don't want to be too tired and miss your hike tomorrow with Nan, do you? You have to get up at six."

"I could stay up for days and days!" said Harry.

"I'm sure you could," said Mum, tucking him in. "But, right now, you need your sleep."

But as soon as Mum had closed the door, Harry
was up again.

"We're going to Dino World," he announced to his
dinosaurs, "where we can stay awake for as long
as we like!"

And with a "One, two, three, jump!" Harry jumped
right into his magical bucket.

"I'm on my way to Dino World!"

But when Harry got there,
Dino World was fast asleep.
"This is no fun!" Harry said to the dinosaurs.
Then he had an idea.
"I know how to wake everyone up!"

"Live on stage for one
night only, Harry and
his Dinosaur Band!"

Harry and his band
rocked Dino World.
    They startled the Moon.
    They shook Moo Mountain.

But no matter how loud
they were, they couldn't keep
Steggy awake. He needed
his sleep and it was well
past his bedtime!

Suddenly something was running towards them
shouting, "Quiet! Quiet, please!"
It was Harry's alarm clock, and he was very cross.

"Do you know what time it is, Harry?" cried the alarm clock. "Midnight! It's midnight! Which is way past all of your bedtimes."

The alarm clock glared at Harry. "Are you going home to bed?" he asked.

"OK," said Harry . . .

"Right after we've run the Dino World All-Night Marathon!"
Harry ran off, shouting to his dinosaurs, "Last one to the
finish line is a rotten dinosaur egg!"

"That was great, everyone!" Harry said, still full of beans. "Now let's play football!"

This time, even Steggy joined in. Although he was fast asleep, he made a brilliant goalie.

Harry's alarm clock caught up with them.

"Now are you going to bed or not, Harry? It's half past two in the morning!"

Harry had to be up in less than four hours for his hike with Nan.

"Oh, you're no fun!" said Harry grumpily. "I don't need a clock to tell me what to do."

"Is that so?" said the alarm clock. "Fine. I quit. You can wake yourself up in the morning!" And off he stomped.

"Good riddance," Harry called after him. "Now there's nothing to stop us staying up and having fun," said Harry.

But his dinosaurs were all fast asleep!
Harry yawned. "I think I'm a bit sleepy too.
I really don't want to miss that hike."
Harry snuggled down next to Patsy.
"There's nothing to worry about," he said,
closing his eyes. "The alarm clock will wake me up."
But, of course, the alarm clock had gone.

Harry sat bolt upright. He would never be able to wake himself up! He had to find that alarm clock.

Harry whistled to his bed. It swept up Harry and his sleeping dinosaurs and whisked them into the sky.

Soon they were flying high over Dino World, with Harry on the lookout for the alarm clock.

Steggy woke up happily from his long sleep.

"Aaaah!" he yelled, as he saw Dino World far below them.
"What are we doing up here, Harry?"

"Looking for my alarm clock," answered Harry sleepily.
"If I could just . . ."

But Harry couldn't stay awake long enough to land
the bed safely. They crash-landed into a tree.

Harry woke up. They had landed in a place full of sleeping clocks. Snoring loudly under a tree was Harry's alarm clock. "Wake up, Mr Clock," pleaded Harry. "I'm so glad I found you. I need you to come home with me to wake me up for the hike!"

"Why should I give you the time of day?" the alarm clock asked haughtily. "You said you don't need me any more."

It was true. Harry suddenly felt ashamed. "I do need you. I do!" he said.

Harry looked so tired that the alarm clock couldn't help but feel sorry for him.

BRRRINNNG!

At the stroke of six o'clock,
Harry's alarm clock rang.

Taury was the first to wake up.
"OK, everybody.
Rise and shine!" he
called. But Harry
didn't stir.
The dinosaurs
climbed up on to
Harry's bed. There was
only one thing for it . . .

"HARRY!" they all yelled in their most roarsome voices.
Harry jolted awake. "I nearly overslept!" he said.
"Well, maybe next time," said Taury, "you shouldn't
stay up all night."

That was when Nan came into the room.
"Good morning, Harry," she said.
"Ready for a nice long hike?"

Harry jumped out of bed.
"Let's go!"